ABOUT THE AUTHOR

Phyllis Arkle was born and educated in Chester. As well as being the author of six Railway Cat titles she also wrote, *Magic at Midnight*, *Midnight in the Air*, *The Village Dinosaur* and *Two Village Dinosaurs*. Sadly, Phyllis Arkle died in 1997.

The Railway Cat

Phyllis Arkle

Illustrated by Stephanie Hawken

Hodder
Children's
Books

a division of Hodder Headline Limited

Text copyright © 1983 Phyllis Arkle
Illustrations copyright © 1999 Stephanie Hawken

First published in 1983 by Hodder & Stoughton Children's Books

Published in paperback in 1985 by Puffin Books
This paperback edition published in 1999
by Hodder Children's Books

A Catalogue record for this book is available from the
British Library

ISBN 0 340 72777 2

Typeset by Avon Dataset Ltd, Bidford-on-Avon, Warks

Printed and bound in Great Britain by
The Guernsey Press Co. Ltd, Guernsey, Channel Islands

Hodder Children's Books
A Division of Hodder Headline Limited
338 Euston Road
London NW1 3BH

Contents

1

Alfie Has His Breakfast

A high-speed train rushed – Swooo . . . oo . . . osh! – through the local station. In the waiting room Alfie stretched himself in his basket and yawned. That would be the overnight express to London, so it must be about half-past five, he thought. He snuggled down again, glad to have a nice warm bed on such a cold, wintry morning. It wouldn't surprise him if snow fell before very long.

A quarter of an hour or so later, a freight train chugged through the station and Alfie knew it was getting-up time. No use being the railway cat if you couldn't be on duty before the rest of the staff.

Staff – that reminded Alfie. The last two days Hack, the new Leading Railman, hadn't given him his early morning saucer of milk and half-tin of cat food. It was just too bad! Alfie hoped for better luck this morning, otherwise he might be forced to prowl round the village doorsteps in search of a bottle of milk to knock over. But he didn't want to do that.

A leap on to a bench, a quick jump, a scramble through a partly open ventilator and the handsome grey and white striped cat was on the platform.

He ran up the steps to the footbridge, which took him over the lines. (He was far too wise to cross any other way.) He arrived on Platform 1 just as Hack was putting the key into the lock of the staff-room door.

Alfie followed the man into the room.

'Hello, nuisance, you here already?' was Hack's surly greeting.

Alfie Has His Breakfast

'Miaow! Miaow! Miaow!' cried Alfie, as he weaved in and out of the man's legs.

'Well, you can scramble. Be off!' cried Hack. 'I've no time for spoilt cats. Platforms must be swept.' Off he strode to collect a broom.

Alfie was aghast. Sweep the platforms, indeed! What about his, Alfie's, breakfast? Was a cat expected to keep the station clear of mice, *and* be friendly to passengers on an empty stomach? He had feared from the start that there was something unpleasant about this new man.

Swish! Swish! Swish! heard Alfie. He peeped round the door. Hack was taking quick sweeps with a large broom and – with a glance round now and then to make sure no one was looking – pushing the rubbish on to the railway lines.

Might have known! thought Alfie. What a way to sweep a platform! Where's his shovel? Too lazy to go and get it, I suppose.

From outside the station came sounds of Splutter! Plop! Splutter! Plop! Ah, good – that would be Fred, the Chargeman, arriving on his scooter. Right on time as usual. Alfie rushed out to meet his friend.

Fred bent down and tickled Alfie under the chin. Alfie enjoyed this but he didn't, as usual, roll over on his back for more. Lack of food and drink was making him feel rather wobbly.

'Miaow! Miaow! Miaow!' he cried, in what he hoped was a mournful tone.

Fred gave him a puzzled glance. 'Alfie seems a bit off colour this morning,' he said to Brown, the Booking Office Clerk, who had just arrived.

'I thought he wasn't quite himself yesterday,' said Brown as he stroked Alfie.

'Well, I'll have a look at you as soon as possible, Alfie,' Fred promised, 'but duty calls at the moment.'

Most of the passengers arriving for the first train were commuters to London. Alfie knew all the regulars. He strolled about accepting a stroke from one, a rub behind the ears from another and a tickle on the chest from yet another.

Alfie Has His Breakfast

He noticed a tall stranger standing next to Hack on the platform. Alfie sat down between the two men. Always get to know the passengers was his motto.

'How are rehearsals going, sir?' Alfie heard Hack ask the man.

'Oh, not bad, not at all bad,' was the answer. 'Expect we'll manage somehow to be ready for opening night just before Christmas.'

Ah, 'rehearsals', thought Alfie. The man must be an actor working in London for the Christmas season and lodging in the village. Alfie knew several actors, living locally, who regularly used the London trains. The London train drew up at the platform. Doors were opened, passengers crowded in and the doors were slammed. The guard gave a signal and the train moved off.

Next, school children, their breath steaming in the cold air, hurried on to the platform and Alfie had a busy time running from one to the other. He always divided his attention equally as he didn't approve of having favourites. The children waved to him as he ran the full length of the platform alongside the outgoing train.

More local trains arrived and departed and, frequently, express trains thundered through the station. It was nearly ten o'clock before things quietened down, and by that time – my goodness! – Alfie was hungry. He began to feel sorry he'd chased away all the mice! Surely Hack wasn't going to neglect him *again*?

The man was nowhere in sight.

But help was at hand.

'Now, let's have a look at you, Alfie,' said Fred. He bent down and carefully pressed his hand over Alfie's back and legs. 'No injured bones,' he declared. Then he gently opened Alfie's mouth and peered down his throat. 'Can't see anything wrong there either.'

Alfie gave his most pathetic 'Miaow!' and ran off towards the staff room at the end of the platform. He stopped and turned round twice to make sure Fred was following. The staff-room door was open. In went Alfie. He sat down and gazed at an empty saucer on the floor.

'What's this?' said Fred as he picked up the saucer. 'This is *dirty*! It hasn't been used recently.' He put his head round the door and yelled, 'Hack!'

Hack sauntered over. (Oh, don't hurry! thought Alfie.) 'Why didn't you give Alfie his milk and food this morning?' asked Fred.

'No time for cats,' muttered Hack as he shuffled his feet and glared at Alfie.

'Well, you listen to me, Hack,' shouted Fred, his face red with annoyance. 'I'm boss here and *there's always time for Alfie*. Got that? He's one of the staff. *I* feed him in the evenings and you do the same in the mornings. Don't forget again. Give him some milk now – in a clean saucer – and food.' Off went Fred in a huff.

Well satisfied at the turn of events, Alfie watched as Hack, mumbling to himself, poured some milk into a clean saucer and placed it on the floor. While Alfie lapped noisily at the milk, the man took a tin of cat food out of a cupboard – and at last the railway cat was served breakfast.

Soon Alfie felt like a new cat. He diligently licked himself all over, and then gave his ears and long shiny whiskers – not forgetting the spiky hairs above his eyes – an extra wash with his paws.

Ready for any emergency now, he said to himself, as he stepped on to the platform. He growled, 'Brr . . . brr . . . brr . . .' at Hack as he ran between the man's legs, tripping him up.

Swearing loudly, Hack fell flat on his back with his legs in the air. How ridiculous he looks, thought Alfie.

Hack shook his fist and shouted, 'I'll get even with you one day, you'll see!'

'Hack!' shouted Fred from across the lines. 'This is no time to be lying down on the platform. Get on with your work!'

'It's that *cat!*' cried Hack, as he got to his feet. 'He's getting on my nerves. He's . . .'

Alfie didn't wait to hear any more. He decided there was just time to go to the front of the station to see if anything interesting was going on there, before meeting the local branch-line train, due in a few minutes.

2

The Runaway Train

There was only one car parked on the station forecourt. The occupants were one young man who, Alfie guessed, was meeting someone off the next train from London – and two very large dogs. One of the dogs, with tongue hanging loose as he panted loudly, had thrust his head out of the open car window and was staring hard at Alfie.

Alfie bristled. Must keep well clear of those dogs, he thought. He turned to run back into the station when – being well used to train sounds – he heard an *unusual* noise. He glanced back, startled.

On time, the branch-line train was coming round the curve towards the station. Nothing wrong about that. *But* it was travelling far too fast. Whatever was happening? thought Alfie, very worried. It was freezing cold. Perhaps ice had formed on the lines and the train was skidding out of control?

Going at that speed, Alfie knew the train couldn't be halted before it crashed through the buffers right on to the station forecourt!

And, apart from the train, what would happen to the car, which was right in the path of the train? And to the young man, who was reading a newspaper? And to the dogs?

Hardly realizing what he was doing, with the hair round his neck standing on end and his teeth bared, Alfie rushed at the car. Bravely, he sprang up at the car window and spat fiercely at the dogs.

Surprised, the young man looked up quickly as, barking fiercely, both dogs one after the other leapt out of the window and went after Alfie.

The young man's eyes widened in amazement and fright as he saw the yellow front of the branch train coming straight for him. He flung open the car door and jumped clear, just before the runaway train, with a grinding, crunching noise, smashed through the buffers and the barrier fence and careered into the parked car, crushing it into a tangled heap of metal.

Alfie had frantically clawed his way up a drainpipe and crouched down on the station roof. The dogs fled and the young man, in a dazed state, stumbled after them.

From his high vantage point, Alfie watched the scene below. All was confusion. The staff rushed out of the station. Fred ran back into the booking office and could be heard shouting at the top of his voice down the telephone,

'STATION – URGENT. ACCIDENT!'

Peering over the guttering Alfie saw that the driver, still trapped in the engine cab, was waving his arms about and his lips were moving. So *he* can't be badly injured, thought Alfie, relieved. The passengers, unharmed but shaken, were being helped from the train.

Soon the police arrived, then a doctor and an ambulance. Alfie watched intently as the driver was lifted out of the cab. With a broken leg and a sore head, but managing to smile at his mates, he was driven off in the ambulance. Next, the passengers were seen off by Fred in a specially chartered bus.

At last, Fred stood back and mopped his brow. 'Phew! What a day!' he exclaimed.

'Thank goodness no one was seriously injured.' He glanced at the buckled train. 'There will be a lot of clearing up work to be done. The cranes will be along shortly to lift the train. Then we'll have to get rid of all the debris. And, of course, an inquiry will be held to find out the cause of the accident – ice on the track, I suspect.'

Fred looked at the car still underneath the train. 'I noticed a young man and two dogs in the car just before the accident,' he said, puzzled.

'Well, I caught sight of him running after the frightened dogs just before the crash,' said Hack. 'I've told the police.'

'Dogs,' said Fred. He had a sudden disturbing thought. 'Where's Alfie? Is *he* all right?'

Hearing his name, Alfie let out a piteous 'Miaow!' He had managed to scramble up the drainpipe, but he had no intention of risking his neck by sliding down it – especially with those dogs about!

'Ah, there you are, Alfie, safe and sound I

hope,' cried Fred, with a sigh of relief. 'Fetch a ladder, Hack, and I'll bring him down.'

'Bothering about a cat,' said Hack as he went off.

'Sharp!' snapped Fred.

When Hack returned, Fred shinned up the ladder, tucked Alfie under one arm and carried him down carefully.

'Always drawing attention to himself, that cat,' said Hack. 'Beats me why we have to put up with him.'

Fred turned to him. 'Listen to me, Hack, once and for all,' he cried. 'Alfie is the railway cat. He *belongs* here . . .'

He was interrupted by the young man running up with the dogs. (Alfie dug his claws into Fred's jacket!) 'I've found the dogs,' panted the young man. 'They were frightened out of their wits – so was I.'

His eyes rested on the crushed car, then he saw Alfie. 'My goodness!' he cried, 'if it hadn't been for that cat, the dogs and I would have been crushed under the train.'

'Cat? You mean Alfie?' said Fred.

'Yes, Alfie, if that's his name. Saved our lives. He rushed up and spat at the dogs. They jumped out of the car. I wouldn't have got out in time if Alfie hadn't disturbed me . . .' He shook his head at the thought and gazed at Alfie in admiration.

'All's well that ends well,' said Fred, beaming. 'Hear that, Hack? "Bothering about a cat," did I hear you say? Why, he's a hero, our Alfie! The reporters will be along soon. His picture will be in the newspapers. He might even appear on television.'

'Huh!' said Hack, scornfully. 'That cat on television? Whatever next. I can't abide cats – least of all Alfie.'

'Here they come!' cried Fred, as a television van drove up. The crew unloaded cameras and proceeded to film the damaged train, the car, the young man and the staff, including Alfie – especially Alfie!

And reporters from local and national newspapers came along with cameramen, and they took photographs of everything and everyone – especially of Alfie!

Very soon a crane arrived and the lifting process began. More pictures were taken – of Alfie sitting right on top of the crane – and of Alfie beside the mangled car.

'It's all that cat!' cried Hack, exasperated. 'You'd think no one else had done anything.'

Meanwhile, the young man and the dogs were taken home in a police car. (Alfie was thankful to see them go.) Things didn't settle down until late afternoon when Fred went home for a well-earned rest. When he returned in the evening he told Alfie, 'There were pictures of us all on television – and lots more of you than of anyone else, you clever cat. You're famous!'

Alfie just said, 'Miaow!' but for the rest of the evening stalked about with his head and tail held high.

Next morning, the commuters showed Alfie his photographs on front pages of the newspapers.

THE CAT WHO SAVED THREE LIVES WHEN A TRAIN SKIDDED ON ICE

was printed underneath the pictures.

Actually, Alfie couldn't imagine what all the fuss was about.

'If *you* saw a car right in the path of a train, you'd try and do something, wouldn't you?' he wanted to ask everybody. There were times when he got very impatient with people for not understanding cat language. But Alfie purred all day. The only unhappy person on the station was Hack.

'That cat will be so conceited after all the

fuss, there'll be no holding him,' he muttered from time to time.

But, of course, he didn't speak out loud, for Alfie was far too popular with everyone.

Passengers brought presents for Alfie, the hero – a nice morsel of fish perhaps, or a piece of crispy bacon. Soon he was in danger of becoming a fat cat and – it must be admitted – a lazy cat. For instance, one morning as he was squatting on the platform, two mice ran right in front of him almost brushing his whiskers. And he didn't give chase!

Oh, dear! Oh, dear! I can't go on like this, thought Alfie as he glanced guiltily over his shoulder to see if anyone else had noticed the mice.

Someone else had – Hack!

'That cat's getting bone idle!' said Hack to Fred who came up at that moment. 'He's just let two mice run almost across his nose. What he needs is a good prod.' He moved a foot in Alfie's direction.

'Don't dare touch him!' cried Fred. 'I've asked the passengers to stop feeding him.

He'll be quite all right with less food and more exercise.'

Alfie moved his head from side to side as Fred rubbed the soft fur under his chin. He purred with pride when Fred added, 'He's the best railway cat we've ever had.'

It was not long before Alfie was his old active self. First, he cleared the station of several mice that had taken advantage of Alfie's laziness to invade the station. He took his duties seriously again and saw the arrival and departure of every train.

There was never a dull moment.

3

Alfie Is Marooned

It was getting much colder. One day Alfie shivered as he glanced up at the darkening sky. A passenger called out to him, 'It's going to snow soon – mind you keep warm, Alfie.'

Sure enough, next morning Alfie woke to find the station covered in dazzling white snow. He had to lift his paws high as he stepped hesitantly down the platform and over the bridge on his way to the staff room. He opened his mouth wide and let a large cold flake settle on his tongue.

Alfie thought it was great fun. Some children arrived at the station on sledges pulled by grown-ups. Alfie was given a ride up and down the station road. And he didn't object when, occasionally, he was accidentally hit by soft round snowballs, which flew into little pieces all over his fur.

For two weeks it snowed. In spite of Hack's sweeping, the platforms were always covered in dirty slush. Snow-ploughs were at work on the lines. Passengers looked weary because trains were delayed (the actor complained to Hack because he was late for rehearsals) and everybody shook and shivered in the cold.

Worst of all – so far as Alfie was concerned – Fred caught a severe chill and had to stay at home. And, as might be expected, one evening Alfie had no supper and no breakfast next morning. Hack took no notice of him.

Alfie decided to give Hack a sharp reminder of his duties. He waited until a two-coach diesel train, with few passengers aboard, came in. Then when Hack came along, he jumped up, stuck his claws into the man's jacket and hung on for all he was worth.

'Hey – what do you think you're doing?' cried Hack as he tried to shake him off. 'Can't attend to *you* yet.'

Alfie clung on for a time then fell back on to the platform. Hack looked round quickly. No one nearby. He picked Alfie up, thrust him into the train and slammed the door shut.

'That's got rid of you for the time being,' he yelled, as he put a hand to his head. (He looked slightly ashamed of himself!)

A whistle was sounded and the train moved away. Alfie felt bewildered. Although he was the railway cat, he'd never before travelled on a train. He walked down the gangway miaowing at the few people sitting on either side. They looked down, surprised.

'Why! It's Alfie!' cried old Granny Davies.

'What's he doing on the train?' said Farmer Cox.

The guard came along. He laughed when he saw Alfie. 'Come for the ride, have you, Alfie?' he said. 'Well, you'll be nice and warm in here with the passengers.'

'Shall we stop the train and send him back to the station?' someone asked.

'Oh, no, no, no,' said the guard. 'Alfie can travel with me to the terminus – *he* doesn't need a ticket! I'll see he gets back safely.'

'He's miaowing a lot,' said Granny Davies.

'Perhaps he's hungry,' said the farmer.

'Hmmm . . . might well be,' said the guard thoughtfully. 'Fred's away ill and Hack, well – *he's* got a lot on his mind at the moment. Probably hasn't bothered about Alfie. Fred will be furious.'

'Perhaps Alfie would like some tea from my flask,' said Granny Davies, who was sitting, well wrapped up, in the middle of the coach.

'That's a good idea,' said the guard. 'There's a bottle of milk in the van. I'll go and get it.'

He soon returned with the milk and a saucer. Alfie eagerly drank the warm tea and milk. Then another passenger produced a lunch packet. He carefully removed the cheese out of two large sandwiches and offered it to Alfie.

Now if there was one thing Alfie enjoyed almost as much as fish, it was cheese. It's my lucky day, he thought.

'Well, that's settled Alfie,' said the guard smiling. 'I'll tell the driver we've got a V I P on board.' He went forward to the driver's cab.

Alfie had a marvellous time. He felt quite skittish as he leapt over the backs of seats from one lap to another. His head jerked from side to side and his eyes opened wide in amazement as he gazed through the window at the snowy fields, with sheep and cattle huddled against fences and trees bending beneath the weight of snow. It was still snowing hard, a real blizzard.

'Hope we don't get snow-bound,' said Granny Davies nervously.

'Perhaps we shouldn't have left the station,' said a boy.

Just after they had passed over a canal, covered in glassy ice, Alfie noticed that the train was slowing down. Slower and slower it moved until at last it came to a halt. Right in the middle of nowhere, it seemed to Alfie – not a human being, nor a building in sight.

The driver jumped down to examine the track ahead. He returned shaking his head. 'The line's completely blocked by a massive snowdrift,' he announced. 'There's no chance of driving through *that*.'

'I'll have to walk back to the nearest lineside telephone . . .' said the guard promptly.

'Only a quarter of a mile away,' put in the driver.

The guard nodded. 'I'll phone the control office and report that we're stuck.'

Alfie Is Marooned

'We'll have to sit it out until we're rescued,' the driver told the passengers. 'I'll keep the heating going. Can't risk Granny Davies getting a chill.'

'Do you think we'll have to spend the night here?' Granny Davies asked in a trembling voice.

'Very unlikely,' said the guard.

'Last winter we were marooned on our farm for twenty days,' said the farmer.

'Oh, dear!' sighed Granny Davies. (Alfie hoped the farmer had had enough food to last twenty days. *He* didn't think he'd be able to manage so long without food!)

They all cheered as the guard started to make his way carefully along the side of the line. The going was difficult for snow was already building up again over the track, which earlier in the day had been cleared by a snow-plough.

Alfie thought being marooned was great fun. Passengers from the other coach, and the driver joined them. Someone started singing and Alfie helped by miaowing occasionally.

Everyone laughed and encouraged him to do it again.

It wasn't very long before the guard could be seen struggling back through the snow. 'I got through to control,' he reported. 'We must just sit tight and await developments.'

Alfie didn't mind. Everyone was so jolly that time passed very quickly. Suddenly the noise of the engine ceased.

'Hello, what's up?' cried the driver, as he made his way to the cab.

He returned after a time, looking worried. 'The heating's gone off because we have run out of fuel – never happened to me before,' he told them. He glanced at Granny Davies. 'We must keep Granny warm.'

He covered her with his own top coat. Someone produced a scarf, which was wound round her hat. Alfie thought she looked very funny.

But it got colder and colder. Granny Davies started complaining. 'It's my *feet*. Might just as well be in a refrigerator,' she said, her teeth chattering. 'If only my *feet* were warm, I'm sure the rest of me would be all right.' A cardigan was wrapped round her feet and for a time the old lady was quiet. Alfie had curled up on a seat beside the farmer, who was fat and comfortable. Alfie didn't mind the cold, but soon Granny Davies became more and more distressed.

'Just like blocks of ice, my feet,' she moaned.

The guard and driver looked at her in dismay. 'She's going blue in the face,' whispered the guard. 'It would be very serious, at her age, if she caught pneumonia.'

'What a pity we haven't got a hot-water bottle,' said the driver.

'What about Alfie?' said the farmer suddenly.

'Alfie?'

'Yes, Alfie. *He's* as warm as toast. Feel him.'

Everyone laughed as the guard unwound the cardigan from round Granny's feet – and put Alfie there instead!

'See if you can do the trick, old chap,' said the guard, smiling. 'Don't worry, Granny, I'm sure Alfie will keep you warm.'

And he did!

Colour came back into the old lady's cheeks and she beamed at everyone. 'Alfie's much better than a hot-water bottle,' she said. 'He's as good as a warm fur muff!'

Time passed and Alfie stayed quietly on Granny's feet. He dozed off now and then as he half-listened to the murmur of voices round him. He woke up suddenly when everyone stopped talking. A throbbing, whirring noise, which Alfie didn't recognize, could be heard. Could it be a train with snow-plough attached coming to the rescue? Or an aeroplane? The passengers were staring out of the windows and soon Alfie heard them all shouting at once,

'Why, it's a helicopter!'

'Coming to our rescue.'

Alfie leapt off Granny's feet and on to a seat. With his paws on a window ledge he watched the helicopter as it hovered over a field just beyond the railway embankment.

'What a good thing there are no high tension cables near here,' said the guard. 'The helicopter will be able to make a perfect landing.'

As the machine touched ground everyone in the train waved and cheered and Alfie miaowed as loudly as possible. And, in no time at all, it seemed to Alfie, they were all, a few at a time, taken aboard the helicopter and ferried to the airfield a few miles away.

Alfie, with the guard and driver, were last to leave. What a day it had been, he thought. His first train journey, and now a helicopter flight. His only regret was that he hadn't been winched aboard – that would have been very exciting!

He felt dizzy as, held by the guard, he gazed below at the canal and fields. After about ten minutes, he craned his neck to see what looked like his own station far below. But they were passing right over it! Was he ever going to get home?

They landed on the airfield and after a car journey with the guard and driver, Alfie found himself back at his own station. And, in spite of all the adventures, he was pleased to be back. For how could the station be properly managed without the assistance of the railway cat?

'Magnificent cat, Alfie,' the guard said to Hack. 'I'm sure he saved Granny Davies's life.' He stared hard at Hack. '*Don't forget to feed him*,' he added.

Hack snorted. Nevertheless, he led the way to the staff room and fed Alfie. 'You'd better stay in here for the night, it's warmer than the waiting room,' he said gruffly. 'I'll leave the radiator on for you.'

He turned at the door. 'Expect your picture will be in the newspapers again,' he said, as he slammed the door and locked it behind him.

Ah, well, thought Alfie as he curled up in the only comfortable chair, perhaps Hack's bark is worse than his bite.

Next morning, Alfie's picture was in the newspapers.

THE SNOWBOUND CAT WHO SAVED AN OLD LADY'S LIFE

* * *

said the caption. That was an exaggeration, thought Alfie – but it had all been great fun. I'll go for another train trip one day, he promised himself.

4

Hack Has a Fright

Alfie was happy. Fred was back at work. The snow had gone and it was getting near to Christmas. He knew that no trains would run on Christmas Day, so the station would be closed. But he wasn't worried about that.

For as long as he could remember, Fred had come to the station twice on Christmas Day. Each time he had brought with him a dish of turkey. Alfie's mouth watered at the very thought of that tender meat.

Everyone was very cheerful. Even Hack was

seen to smile – once! But Alfie was careful to keep out of the man's way. Christmas was a time of goodwill, and he didn't want to upset Hack again.

One day a group of students dashed off a train as soon as it pulled up at the bay platform. In high spirits they laughed and joked as they made their way to the exit. They stopped to offer a sweet to Alfie. He took it carefully between his teeth before chewing and swallowing it. Not bad, he thought, but he hoped the students didn't think sweets were his favourite food. (Just think of Fred's turkey!) Still, it was kind of the boys.

Fred appeared. He smiled at the students. 'Don't give Alfie too many sweets. He'll be getting fat again,' he said.

Several students spoke at the same time.

'Oh, no, no, no . . . we won't do that.'

'We'd . . . er . . . better be going.'

'Yes, let's scram!'

They seemed very excited as, laughing and jostling one another, they went through the exit and ran down the road.

Fred stroked his chin. 'Hmmm . . .' he said, 'I wonder why they are in such a hurry?'

Alfie decided to stroll across to the bay platform to find out if a crisp or two, or a sweet had been left behind in the train. He knew that the train, its doors wide open, standing at the platform wasn't due out for another twenty minutes.

He jumped in and started to search the first coach by leaping on to all the seats and then crawling underneath them. But, apart from a couple of newspapers and a sweet paper with not a trace of sticky sugar left on it, Alfie drew a blank.

He'd just emerged from under the last seat when – what was that? He froze in horror – his fur stood on end and he felt as prickly as a porcupine. With one paw in the air, and tail quivering, he stared at a great hairy monster, with massive shoulders and staring eyes, which was slumped between two seats.

Alfie stood rigid for at least half a minute. He was about to turn and rush out of the train in terror, when he noticed something which made him stop. The beast's eyes in its black and wrinkled face didn't flicker and its long arms hung limply.

Was the monster ill? Overcoming his fright, Alfie crept forward on his stomach. He put out a paw and touched the beast's leg, before springing back warily – but the animal didn't move. Alfie waited a moment, then he went nearer and looked into the marble-like eyes.

Then Alfie understood – the thing was *stuffed*. Now what on earth was a strange thing like a stuffed animal doing in a train at Alfie's

station? He knew that cheque books, credit cards and pocket calculators – and umbrellas! – among other things, were often left in trains, but this beat everything!

Just then Alfie heard Hack shouting to someone as he approached the bay platform. Goodness, I don't think Hack's very brave. He's going to get the shock of his life (and be more bad-tempered than ever) if he comes on this monster unawares. Alfie was worried.

How could he warn Hack? He thought for a moment, then he crept, out of sight, under the animal's slightly raised left arm. As Hack came abreast of the train, Alfie filled his lungs before letting out a hideous howling noise. He felt quite proud of his efforts, so he did it again – and again. That should warn Hack, who would probably go running for Fred, and nothing ever scared Fred.

However, startled but curious, Hack stepped cautiously into the train and made his way slowly down the coach, searching the seats, the luggage racks and, occasionally, bending down to glance under the seats.

Just before Hack sighted the monster, Alfie howled again. (Better than before, he thought!) Shocked and unable to believe his eyes or his ears, Hack halted. Rooted to the spot, he gazed and gazed at the beast confronting him. Alfie, still out of sight, moved and the animal appeared to raise its arm slightly.

This was too much for Hack. Shrieking 'Ahh . . . ahhhaaa . . . aaa . . . aaa . . . !' he rushed down the gangway, leapt out of the train – and bumped right into Fred.

'Hey there, look where you're going!' cried Fred. 'Whatever's the matter?'

Hack gulped. He had difficulty in speaking. 'It . . . it . . . it's in . . . in *there*.' He gulped again and waved a shaking arm towards the train.

'*What's* in there?' asked Fred, irritated.

'A . . . a . . . terr . . . if . . . ific thing, a mon . . . mon . . . mon . . . monster!'

'Don't be silly – you've been dreaming!' cried Fred, as he took hold of Hack by the shoulders and shook him.

At this moment Alfie howled again. (He was quite enjoying himself.)

'Listen – that's it!' gasped Hack. He turned to flee, but Fred clutched his arm and held him back.

'No running away. We're on duty – remember,' he said sternly. 'Come on, show me the monster.'

Still holding on to Hack, he boarded the train. By now, Brown and several other people had arrived to find out what all the noise was about. They all trooped into the train.

Fred's eyes widened and he gasped in surprise when he saw the monster. He drew back hastily. Then, squaring his shoulders, he leaned forward and peered at the beast. He burst out laughing as he caught sight of two round green eyes staring at him from underneath the monster's hairy arm.

'Thought so!' he cried. 'Come out, Alfie. Let Hack take a look at you.'

Obligingly Alfie jumped clear and the beast's arm fell back into position.

'You're right, Hack,' cried Fred, choking

with mirth, 'it is a monster – of sorts. It's a stuffed *gorilla*!'

Everyone, except Hack, thought it was hilarious, but Hack shuffled his feet and scowled at Alfie.

'Oh, dear! Oh, dear! I feel helpless with laughing,' cried Fred, as he clung to the back of a seat. 'Who would have thought our Alfie could make a noise which would frighten Hack nearly out of his wits?'

Hack was very put out. 'That cat's always trying to take the mickey out of me,' he shouted. 'I shan't forget this in a hurry.'

'Now, now, calm down, Hack,' said Fred. 'No harm's been done and I'm sure Alfie was only trying to be helpful.'

Hack shouted, 'Helpful? Him? He's as helpful as a cartload of monkeys.'

'What I'm wondering,' put in Brown, 'is how did the gorilla get into the train?'

Fred had an answer. 'Remember the students coming off the train earlier on? Well, I wondered why they made off in such a hurry. My guess is that they stole the gorilla from a museum – or from a private collection, perhaps – just for a lark. Then they didn't know what to do with it, so left it on the train.'

'Well, I must say it was very clever of them to get it out of a museum without being detected, and then on to a train without anyone noticing,' said Brown.

Fred nodded. 'There'll be a row about this,' he said. 'Railway staff and museum staff will have to be more on the alert in future. Still – it's getting near to Christmas and I suppose students, like most people, are feeling light-hearted . . .'

In the event, the students got a good ticking off from various quarters and promised never to do such a thing again. But Alfie thought that, if he knew anything about students, it wouldn't be long before they got up to more mischief. He must practise making hideous noises in case they came in useful!

Everyone, except Hack, liked talking about the gorilla. But Hack walked about with a frown on his face, which deepened whenever he caught sight of Alfie.

Alfie sighed. After all, he'd only tried to save Hack from getting a shock. But, he had to admit, he *had* enjoyed making those wonderful gorilla noises –

5

A Trip to London

It was only ten days to Christmas. Alfie watched mothers going by train to a nearby town and returning laden with Christmas shopping. He listened to children talking excitedly about school plays, parties and presents. He could hardly wait for Christmas.

'Looking forward to the turkey, Alfie?' Fred would ask jokingly.

Only Hack went about with never a smile on his face. One morning when Alfie was standing by the actor, who was waiting for a

London train, Hack came up suddenly. (Alfie decided that it would be undignified to dash off, so he stayed where he was and listened. In any case, Alfie was still waiting for his breakfast.)

'Good morning, Hack,' said the actor pleasantly, as he breathed in deeply. 'It's a nice, crisp day, isn't it?' He stared at Hack. 'I wonder why you always look so, well, er . . . sort of glum?'

Hack muttered something under his breath, then he turned and saw Alfie. '. . . and that cat, always getting in the way, always wanting food,' (not true, thought Alfie) 'always showing off,' (Really!) 'and I haven't forgotten how he made a fool of me with his imitation gorilla noises.' (And very good noises they were, said Alfie to himself.)

The actor gazed at Alfie as if he'd never seen him before. 'He's a fine, handsome, beautifully marked cat . . .' he said, thoughtfully.

'Miaow!' said Alfie, very pleased that Hack was listening.

'. . . I wonder? Hack! I've just had a

marvellous idea. The pantomime is due to start tomorrow night – and we're in a right fix. We could do with a live cat. I think Alfie would solve the problem. I'll take him with me if you like.'

'Take him? Will you, really?' said Hack eagerly. He looked round guiltily to make sure Fred wasn't in sight. 'But he hasn't been fed yet.'

'All the better for that,' said the actor. He held out a canvas bag. 'Quick! Slip him in

here. No one's taking any notice. They're all reading the morning papers.'

Before Alfie had time to realize what was happening, Hack swooped down, picked him up and popped him into the bag. The train came in and Alfie wailed loudly as he was carried into a compartment. He struggled and scratched the inside of the bag when he felt the train move off.

Alfie had never been shut up like this before, and he complained bitterly at the loss of his self-respect. He was very worried. Whatever had the actor meant when he had said it was all the better that Alfie hadn't been fed? And what did he want with a cat - a *live* cat – anyhow? Alfie moaned loudly as he kicked and scratched again.

'What have you got in there?' he heard a man ask.

'Oh, it's only my son's cat. I'm taking him to London for a check-up.'

What lies, thought poor Alfie. To add to his miseries, he began to feel he was suffocating, and was very relieved when the bag was opened about an inch. He tried with all his strength to claw his way out.

But the actor patted the bag reassuringly. 'Keep quiet, Alfie,' he whispered. 'We'll soon be in London.'

At the third stop the actor (and Alfie) left the train. Alfie guessed by the noise and bustle – much much louder than at his own station – that they must be at the London railway terminus. He'd always wanted to visit London, but he might just as well have been in a small stuffy cave for all he could see.

The actor hailed a taxi. 'To the Dolphin Theatre,' he said. He jumped in and carefully put the bag beside him on the seat.

'Nearly there, Alfie,' he said.

The bag, with Alfie inside, swayed as the driver swerved and braked in the traffic. Alfie didn't think he'd have much chance of finding his way home through the London traffic, even if he managed to escape from the actor.

Soon they arrived at the theatre.

'The producer wants to see you urgently, sir,' said the doorkeeper as they entered the building through the stage door. 'He's got the jitters,' he added.

'I'll cure his jitters,' said the actor smiling. He went down a passage towards the stage.

'Oh, thank goodness you've arrived!' exclaimed the producer. 'We're in real trouble. The "cat" man is still off ill and, worse still, we can't find a replacement anywhere. We've tried the agencies, but all suitable actors are booked for the Christmas season. We can't possibly do the show without a *cat*.'

'He's in here,' said the actor, laughing.

'*Who's* in *where*?' said the producer, puzzled.

'Alfie. In the bag. I suggest we use a real live cat instead of a man dressed up as a cat. The children will love Alfie, and I'm sure we'll be able to train him at rehearsal tonight in time for the opening tomorrow.'

'Phew!' said the producer, wiping his forehead. 'I hope you're right. Let's have a look at him.'

'Come along to my dressing room. Can't risk him escaping,' said the actor.

Thankfully Alfie jumped out of the bag as

soon as it was opened. He found himself in a small room. The first thing he noticed was a large mirror over a wide dressing table. On the table were jars, tubes and brushes. Hung on hooks round the walls were fancy costumes and hats. Several pairs of boots and shoes were on the floor.

'Well, what do you think of Alfie?' asked the actor.

'He's certainly a fine-looking animal,' was the reply, 'but do you *really* think he'll be able to play the part?'

'Certainly he will – with a little "fishy" help, of course!' laughed the actor.

'Well . . . we'll see,' said the producer doubtfully. 'In any case, he's our only hope. You'd better get dressed. I'll call a rehearsal to begin in an hour's time.'

'I'll be ready,' said the actor. 'Will you send someone for milk and fish for *after* the show, and a basket?'

After the producer had left, the actor said, 'I'm relying on you to do your best, Alfie.'

Now Alfie always believed in doing his best

in everything, but what was he supposed to be doing his best for in this case?

'First, you'll have some milk,' the actor went on, 'and, later on, some fish. What more could you want?'

'Miaow! Miaow! Miaow!' wailed Alfie, which meant, 'I want to go straight back to my railway station.'

However, being a sensible cat, as well as a clever one, he decided there was nothing he could do for the time being, but obey orders.

There was a knock on the door and a man entered with a bottle of milk, a paper-wrapped parcel of fish (Alfie could smell it!) and a wide, flat basket.

'Here you are, Alfie,' said the actor, as he poured some milk into a saucer and put it on the floor in front of Alfie. When Alfie had finished lapping up the milk, he said, 'Miaow!' which meant, 'I'm ready for the fish now.'

But he wasn't given any fish! The parcel had been placed on a high shelf so, with his eyes, Alfie measured the distance from floor to a chair, and then from chair to shelf. He got ready to spring, but the actor put out a hand.

'It's not time for the fish yet, Alfie,' he said. 'You'll have to be patient until *after the show.*'

After the show? What did that mean, thought Alfie. Why, he hadn't had a bite to eat since Fred had given him his supper last evening! The thought of Fred – and of the turkey he might never taste -made Alfie feel very sad. He miaowed quietly.

'Oh, don't worry, everything will be all right, Alfie,' said the actor, kindly. 'Just do as I tell you and you'll get your fish eventually.'

The man started to dress for the show, in ragged clothes. Then he made a few more rags into a bundle, which he tied to the end of a stick. He was barefooted and looked like a poor waif. Alfie was puzzled, until the actor explained.

'Listen carefully, Alfie. In the pantomime, *I'm* Dick Whittington and *you're* my cat.' He stretched up and took the parcel of fish from the shelf. 'You're going to follow this fish about the stage. If I'm holding it, you follow me. If another actor has it, you follow him. Understand?'

'Miaow!' said Alfie. He didn't really understand why he couldn't have the fish before the show, but he was ready to do his best and the thought of supper spurred him on.

The actor bent down and fastened a collar and lead round Alfie's neck. Alfie was outraged. He struggled wildly and made angry noises.

'Now, now, that's enough,' cried the actor.

'It's only for the rehearsal. I'm sure you'll be able to act without the collar and lead in the real performance.'

He led Alfie out of the room and down a corridor towards the back of the stage. The lights were dazzling and the noise almost deafening. There were so many people standing about, some in costume and others in ordinary working clothes, that Alfie felt quite bewildered.

But everyone seemed pleased to see Alfie, and to admire him.

'He's a very handsome cat.'

'Quite a character, I should imagine.'

'Best of luck, Alfie. Don't let us down.'

'He won't let us down. He'll steal the show if we're not careful!'

And – to start with – Alfie *did* steal the rehearsal.

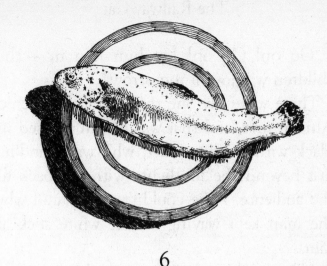

6

Alfie Follows the Fish

From the moment it was Alfie's turn to go on
stage he was a sensation. With head held high
he stepped proudly after Dick Whittington
(and the fish!) without having to be pulled.
He looked round with interest, and when the
chorus started singing, Alfie opened his
mouth, threw back his head and joined in.

'Miao . . . aow . . . aow . . . iaow!'

Everybody laughed so much that the
rehearsal had to stop. The producer, wiping
tears of mirth from his eyes, called out.

'Go on! Go on! Let him join in – the children will love it tomorrow.'

There was only one thing which bothered Alfie at first, and that was a man dressed in black with a white shirt, who was standing just beyond the footlights with his back to the audience. Alfie couldn't understand why the man kept waving a little white stick at him.

Alfie didn't approve of sticks being waved at anyone! So the first time he got close enough to the footlights, he craned his neck and hissed loudly at the conductor of the orchestra. He even -although he knew it wasn't good manners – spat at him once! To Alfie's surprise, everyone burst out laughing again and the rehearsal came to a halt.

'Oh, do get on with it, please,' implored the producer. 'It's fine – just fine. Alfie will have the children jumping about with excitement.'

So the rehearsal continued, and Alfie began to understand what the play was about. It appeared that Dick Whittington, the ragged hungry waif, who had come to London to

seek his fortune, didn't find the London streets paved with gold as he had been led to believe. Instead, he had to work for a cook who scolded and beat him all the time. He was made to sleep in an attic overrun with rats and mice.

And that was where Alfie came in. Dick bought him in a market for *one penny*. (What an insult, thought Alfie. He was glad Hack wasn't about – still, it was only a story.)

Alfie followed Dick (and the fish!) about the stage. He got rid of all the rats and mice in Dick's attic bedroom. To his disgust, they were battery-operated rats and mice!

Dick badly needed money, so he gave Alfie to a sea captain to sell for him. But Dick was so unhappy because he had sent his cat away, that he decided to run away himself. But the bells of Bow Church rang out and seemed to be singing,

'Turn again, Whittington,
Lord Mayor of London,
Turn again, Whittington,
Thrice Mayor of London.'

so Dick turned back.

Meanwhile, Alfie followed the sea captain (and the fish!) and soon cleared the ship of hundreds of rats and mice. When they arrived at a far country, they found the king's palace overrun with rats and mice too. (What a lot of rats and mice there were in this pantomime world, thought Alfie. If only they were *real!*) Anyway, Alfie chased them all out of the kingdom.

The king was so pleased with alfie that he gave the sea captain a *casket full of gold and jewels* to take back to Dick Whittington in payment for his cat. (Alfie wouldn't have minded Hack hearing about this.) So Alfie stayed in the far country and followed the king (and the fish!) while the sea captain sailed back to London with the casket.

The gold and jewels made Dick Whittington a very rich man and, as Bow Bells had foretold, he became Lord Mayor of London, not once, but three times. And all because of his cat – that's *me*, thought Alfie. He was very pleased that everything had turned out so well, even if it was only make-believe.

The producer and the cast were all full of praise for Alfie and all agreed he was the star of the show.

'He can't put a paw wrong,' said the producer.

Alfie was glad he'd given satisfaction, but he was getting hungrier and hungrier. Eventually he followed the actor (and the fish!) back to the dressing room, and at last – at long last! – the railway cat had his supper.

Later on he settled down in the basket. The actor told him, 'I'm going home now, Alfie. You'll be quite comfortable here. The night watchman will look in on you during the night.' Off he went.

Alfie knew the actor would be travelling by train to Alfie's own railway station, where Fred would be on duty to meet the late night train. How Alfie longed to see Fred again. He wouldn't mind even seeing Hack as well.

For the next few days – every evening (except Sunday) and two matinees – Alfie took part in the pantomime – without the collar and lead. He had no food until after the evening shows. He was definitely a hit. The children loved him and cheered and clapped whenever he appeared. The show played to packed houses as news of Alfie's success spread.

Alfie enjoyed it at first, but gradually he became restless. This was no job for a railway cat. His thoughts turned more and more to his real life on the station – the staff, passengers, happy children, and Granny Davies on her way to visit her daughter for Christmas. Sadly, Alfie hoped they were all missing him.

One afternoon – just two days before Christmas – Alfie followed the fish on to the stage as usual. There were hundreds of children in the audience and they gave Alfie a rapturous reception. This particular afternoon, after the applause had died down, he heard a shrill voice in the audience calling out.

'But it *is* Alfie. I'm sure it is!'

'Ssh! Ssh! Ssh!' came from all sides.

'*But it is . . .*'

'Quiet, please,' shouted someone, and the shrill young voice was heard no more. Apparently no one on stage, except Alfie, had heard.

Alfie had difficulty in concentrating on his

part in the show. Had someone really recognized him? Was he going to be rescued? Afterwards, resting in the dressing room between shows, he was excited – and hopeful. Unable to settle down, he got up and started to prowl round the room.

'What's the matter, Alfie?' asked the actor, who had been reading a newspaper. 'I hope you're not sickening for something. That would be a pity after your success in the show.'

'Miaow!' said Alfie. He didn't care about success. Only about getting back to his station.

During the evening show he went as near to the footlights as he dared, in case anyone recognized him again. But no one shouted, 'It *is* Alfie!' and his spirits sank.

Back in the dressing room he ate his supper without any real enjoyment. He ate to keep up his strength, for he was determined that if he wasn't rescued very soon, he would try to escape . . .

But suddenly there was a peremptory knock, the door burst open and in walked – Fred! Alfie stared for a moment, unable to believe his eyes. Then he made a mad rush. Fred picked him up and hugged him hard. Alfie purred and purred and purred – and *purred*. He'd never felt so relieved and happy in all his life.

'My word, Alfie, it is *good* to see you,' sighed Fred. 'Young Ted Asprey told me he was certain he'd seen you in the show. I caught the very next train. I hear you've been a terrific success but . . .' He turned to the actor, who sat in a chair, with make-up still on his face.

'As for *you*,' shouted Fred. 'Listen. Alfie is

not a pantomime cat, and never will be. He's our *railway cat*. Don't forget that again, or I'll . . . I'll . . . I'll have the *law* on you.'

The actor looked very crestfallen. 'I'm sorry – I didn't stop to think . . .'

'Well, you should think!' cried Fred, scornfully.

'But we were in such trouble because we couldn't find anyone to play the cat. I thought it was a brilliant idea to have Alfie. He could earn thousands of pounds as a stage cat,' said the actor.

'Miaow!' growled Alfie, and hissed.

'He's *not a stage cat*,' roared Fred. 'You'd better watch out, or else . . .'

The actor shrank back in his chair. 'All right, all right,' he said hastily. 'I've said I'm sorry and you can see for yourself that Alfie has come to no harm.'

He sighed heavily. 'I really don't know what we're going to do without him. I'm afraid the show will have to close and we'll all be out of a job.'

'That's your problem,' said Fred.

Alfie was beginning to feel just a bit sorry for the man (after all he had been kind), and for the rest of the cast, when there was a rap on the door and in walked the producer.

He looked from one to the other. 'What's the matter?' he asked.

'We're in trouble again,' sighed the actor. 'Fred insists on taking Alfie back with him.'

'Alfie is our railway cat, and you had no right to take him away,' said Fred, his voice trembling with indignation.

The producer turned to the actor. 'You didn't tell me Alfie came here without the owner's permission,' he said.

'I thought no one would mind,' said the actor miserably, 'and now Alfie's going, we'll all be out of work.'

'Well, as a matter of fact we won't,' said the producer. 'The actor who was originally cast as the cat is better. He's reporting for duty tomorrow, so we don't really need Alfie.'

Alfie felt very pleased about this but Fred shouted, 'That doesn't alter the fact that Alfie was, well – catnapped as you might say.'

'No, it doesn't,' agreed the producer, 'and
you must be compensated. I cannot afford to
pay gold and jewels for his services.' He
grinned. 'But will one hundred pounds settle
the matter?'

'One hundred pounds?' cried Fred. 'That's
too . . . no, no, no it isn't too much. Alfie's
worth every penny – and more. The money
will go to the Railway Benevolent Fund. Suit
you, Alfie?'

'Miaow!' said Alfie, pushing his head under
Fred's chin.

'So that's settled,' said the producer, 'but
we'll never have another actor like Alfie. It
was a great experience working with him.'

'It really was,' agreed the actor. He looked
at his watch. 'Goodness!
I didn't realize
it was so late,' he said. 'I won't be able to
remove my make-up in time to catch the last
train, so I'll stay here for the night. You'd
better hurry, Fred.'

Fred nodded. 'Coming, Alfie?' he said.

Coming? Of course he was coming. Alfie

Alfie Follows the Fish

wouldn't let Fred go home without him for all
the fish in the sea!

7

The Turkey – and More

The producer ordered a taxi, and Alfie left
the theatre clinging to Fred's shoulder. He
had no intention of removing his claws from
Fred's jacket until he reached his own station.
They caught the train just in time.

'Nothing but the best for Alfie,' said the
guard as, with a flourish, he opened the door
of a first-class compartment and ushered them
in.

Fred talked to Alfie. The passengers talked
to him. And Alfie purred all the way home.

And – what a surprise! – late as it was, news of Alfie's homecoming had gone round the village. It seemed to him that half the population had turned out to welcome him. Brown came on his bicycle, but there was no sign of Hack.

Several children had been allowed to stay up. They pushed and struggled to take turns at stroking Alfie. Suddenly he heard a voice among all the hubbub of conversation.

'*I* saw you first, in the theatre this afternoon, Alfie. *I* told Fred you were there,' and a small boy pushed his way to the front.

Alfie stretched out his front legs and then rolled over and over. 'Miaow! Miaow! Miaow!' he cried, by way of thanks.

It was well after midnight before everyone, except Fred, went home. Fred stayed behind to give Alfie a saucer of milk, and to settle him in his basket in the waiting room.

'You wouldn't believe how much we've missed you – even Hack, I think!' he said. 'But *I'll* make sure you get your breakfast tomorrow.' He bent down to stroke Alfie.

'Good night, Alfie. Sleep well.'

Alfie promptly fell asleep. He dreamt he heard bells (Bow Bells?) and imagined he saw a casket full of gold and silver and jewels, otherwise his sleep was undisturbed. He didn't wake up until the early-morning freight train chugged through the station.

He lost no time in making his way to the staff room to wait for Fred, but – surprise! surprise! – Hack's first duty was to feed Alfie. More surprising still, he even smiled – a lop-sided sort of smile, but a smile nevertheless.

Alfie could hardly believe it – had Hack turned over a new leaf, or was he afraid of being found out about his part in Alfie's disappearance?

After his meal, Alfie cleaned his fur, spruced his whiskers and prepared to greet the commuters, the children, the shoppers . . . He sighed contentedly. Really, life at his own station on Christmas Eve was very satisfying.

The station was busy all day. Nearly everybody cried 'Merry Christmas!' and sometimes, 'Merry Christmas, Alfie – so glad you're back. The station wouldn't be the same without you.'

At last it was time for the station to be closed, the lights to be extinguished and for Fred to go home. Alfie went to bed. There was no early morning train to wake him up on Christmas morning, so he had an extra lie-in.

When he did wake up, his first duty was to patrol the station twice, to make sure everything was in order. He knew Fred would be arriving soon with his breakfast turkey, and he could hardly contain his excitement.

To while away the waiting time, he frisked and frolicked along the platform, over the bridge and back again, chasing imaginary rats and mice. Suddenly, his sharp ears caught the sound of a key being turned stealthily in the entrance gate lock. That wasn't Fred! Fred always opened the door noisily, especially on Christmas mornings, and shouted,

'Alfie! You there, Alfie?'

Alfie crouched underneath the steps leading to the bridge. Up the other steps on the

opposite platform crept a tall figure dressed
in a red cloak and a red and white cap with a
tassel on it. He had a long snowy-white beard
and was carrying a sack over one shoulder.

Red cloak, white beard, sack – it must be a
man dressed up as Father Christmas. How
jolly, thought Alfie. He started to rush
forward to meet this unexpected but welcome
figure, when he stopped as a thought struck
him.

Why was the man visiting the station on
Christmas *Day* instead of Christmas *Eve*? Alfie
sat down again, and waited. He watched the
man walk over the bridge and down the steps.
As he drew nearer, Alfie noticed that the man
wore a mask. His eyes, through the slits,
glanced furtively this way and that. Someone
up to no good, thought Alfie. Now what . . . ?

The answer came to him suddenly. The man
must be a burglar! He'd probably gone to an
all-night party disguised as Father Christmas,
and had come away with the loot – gold, jewels
and silver ornaments, probably. Something
heavy inside the sack clanked now and then

as the man approached Alfie's hiding place.

Alfie was certain the burglar intended hiding the sack somewhere on the station. Then, next morning, he would come along with an empty suitcase, pick up the goods and catch the first fast train to London. What a very good detective I would make, thought Alfie.

He tensed his muscles, clenched his paws and sprang. Taken by surprise, the man lost his balance and crashed heavily on to the platform. The sack caught him a sharp blow on the side of the head as he fell.

Muffled groans and screams could be heard coming from behind the mask as the man struggled to shake Alfie off his back. But Alfie had no intention of releasing him until Fred arrived. Every time the man tried to get to his feet, Alfie snarled, hissed, unsheathed his claws and threatened to bite and scratch.

Alfie hoped Fred would hurry up as he couldn't keep this up much longer. Soon, to his relief, he heard the gate opening and the familiar voice calling.

'Alfie! You there, Alfie?'

'*Miaow! Miaow! Miaow!*' howled Alfie.

Carrying a foil-covered dish in one hand, Fred rushed over the bridge and down the steps. He stared in amazement at the figure lying on the platform.

'Whatever's going on?' he wanted to know. 'What *are* you doing to Father Christmas, Alfie?'

But, to Alfie's surprise, Fred was laughing. 'Get up, Father Christmas,' he ordered. 'I'd recognise those eyes anywhere!'

Slowly the man rose to his feet.

'Now you'd better unmask,' said Fred, with a grin.

'No, no . . . I'll be getting off home,' muttered the man .

'Oh, no, you won't. Take it off, or shall I do it for you?' cried Fred.

'Oh, all right, all right,' said the man irritably.

Off came the mask and there stood – Hack! Alfie was so amazed that he couldn't even miaow.

Hack was very annoyed. 'That cat . . .' he began.

'Now, now, don't forget it's Christmas Day, a time for tolerance and goodwill,' Fred reminded him. 'But do tell Alfie and me *why* you've come to the station on Christmas Day dressed up as Father Christmas?'

Hack looked at the ground and shuffled his feet. Then he burst out, 'Well, if you want to know the truth, I'm tired of that cat giving me fright after fright *and* making a fool of me. I thought, just for a change, I'd turn the tables on him, creep up and scare the daylight out of him. Only a joke really. There was no need for him to attack me . . .'

'Alfie only *pretended* to attack you. He probably thought you were a trespasser or a burglar and it was up to him to do his duty.'

'Miaow!' said Alfie.

'I think it's time you two called a truce – at least for Christmas,' Fred went on.

'Miaow!' said Alfie again.

'I suppose so,' said Hack, grudgingly.

'That's settled then,' said Fred, beaming. 'And it's high time Alfie had his Christmas breakfast.' He started to take the foil off the dish.

'Just a minute,' said Hack.

He picked up the sack, turned it upside down, shook it, and out fell – not gold or jewels or precious stones – but four tins of cat meat and two tins of lobster soup!

'Christmas present for Alfie,' said Hack, with a sidelong grin at Fred.

'Well, well, well, what do you think about that, Alfie?' said Fred. 'Aren't you a lucky cat?'

Alfie looked up at Hack, then he rolled over and over on his back, with his paws tucked up and his head back. Fred laughed out loud and Hack, well . . . he *almost* smiled.

Fred ripped off the foil. 'Turkey for Alfie now,' he said. 'You can start on the tinned food tomorrow.'

Alfie set to and – my goodness! – the turkey was so good, if not better than ever. Meanwhile, Hack picked up the tins and put them back into the sack. 'I'll bring them along tomorrow,' he promised. Fred and Hack waited until he had finished, then Alfie accompanied them as far as the gate. (He was the only one on duty today, he thought, proudly.)

'See you later, Alfie,' said Fred. He waved

his hand. Alfie saw him nudge Hack, who rather reluctantly lifted an arm slightly, as if he *might* manage a wave, if he tried very hard.

Alfie laughed to himself. It was a very pleasant and unexpected feeling to have a wave from Hack on Christmas Day, even if it was only half a wave!

Alfie thought about the truce. Perhaps Hack had got used to him, even liked him – a little – or . . . but, never mind, he wouldn't bother about Hack until after Christmas.

Instead, he'd think of Fred (and the turkey) and about his duties as the railway cat.

By Phyllis Arkle

The Railway Cat's Secret

Fred has a secret – and whatever it is, it's making Alfie's life a misery. Fred has no time for a chat any more.

Then Alfie discovers a little station, further down the track – with it's own special secret! Alfie is determined not to let anyone find it – but then some unexpected visitors arrive and nobody has a secret any more . . .

By Phyllis Arkle

The Railway Cat and the Ghost

Alfie the Railway Cat is feeling unloved. A holiday at Hill Top Farm is just what he needs. But somebody's out to spoil his fun.

What can Alfie do to get his own way? Farmer Jones may have the perfect solution . . .

By Phyllis Arkle

The Railway Cat and the Horse

An important arrival is expected at the station – Alfie and the villagers are intrigued, and very excited when they discover it is a horse. Could it be a racehorse!

But this horse is not only important, it's valuable too. Alfie volunteers to help keep an eye on it. But has he taken on more than he bargained for . . ?

THE RAILWAY CAT

0 340 67288 9	THE RAILWAY CAT'S SECRET	£3.50 ☐
0 340 69993 0	THE RAILWAY CAT AND THE GHOST	£3.50 ☐
0 340 73214 8	THE RAILWAY CAT AND THE HORSE	£3.50 ☐

All Hodder Children's books are available at your local bookshop, or can be ordered direct from the publisher. Just tick the titles you would like and complete the details below. Prices and availability are subject to change without prior notice.

Please enclose a cheque or postal order made payable to *Bookpoint Ltd*, and send to: Hodder Children's Books, 39 Milton Park, Abingdon, OXON OX14 4TD, UK.
Email Address: orders@bookpoint.co.uk

If you would prefer to pay by credit card, our call centre team would be delighted to take your order by telephone. Our direct line *01235 400414* (lines open 9.00 am–6.00 pm Monday to Saturday, 24 hour message answering service). Alternatively you can send a fax on *01235 400454*.

TITLE		FIRST NAME		SURNAME	

ADDRESS	
DAYTIME TEL:	POST CODE

If you would prefer to pay by credit card, please complete:
Please debit my Visa/Access/Diner's Card/American Express (delete as applicable) card no:

Signature... Expiry Date ....

If you would NOT like to receive further information on our products please tick the box. ☐